DAS

The Panda Bear From China

and

The Snowflake

ISBN 978-1-0980-4276-9 (paperback)
ISBN 978-1-0980-4277-6 (digital)

Christian Faith Publishing, Inc.
832 Park Avenue
Meadville, PA 16335
www.christianfaithpublishing.com

Printed in the United States of America

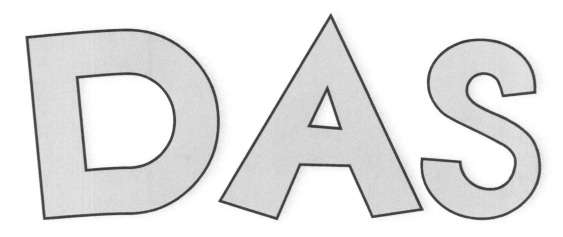

DAS

The Panda Bear From China

and

The Snowflake

Suzie Marie

Das is a seven-year-old panda bear who lives in China with his mom, dad, brother, and sister, oh we almost forgot about his pet dog too.

He likes living in China, but sometimes during the winter, it gets really, really cold, and when it gets really, really cold, it snows.

Das plays a fun game: when he sees snowflakes, he likes to catch the snowflakes on his tongue.

Sometimes, he misses and it goes right on his face, but it doesn't hurt at all.

Das likes to make believe and pretend he can catch a snowflake in his hands and make a wish and maybe the wish will come true.

One day, when it was snowing, Das caught a really big snowflake in his hands and made a wish.

He wished he had more friends at recess, so he could learn and play new games.

The next day, he asked someone new to be his friend, and they both played new games. He was happy that wish came true.

The next time it snowed, Das went outside to catch a snowflake in his hands.

He saw a really big snowflake and waited for it to float down.

After his caught it, he made a wish that he and his family could have fun and play games and climb trees at the local park.

On Saturday, his wish came true; everyone sure had a lot of fun.

Once in while, Das would catch a snowflake in his hands and make a wish that someone who was sick would feel better soon and would be able to play outside just like he can.

He would tell all his friends to catch a snowflake and make a wish for their family to be nice and happy.

So every time it snows, Das makes a point to catch as many snowflakes as possible and make as many wishes so every one is as happy as he is.

So even if it's NOT snowing, all you need is a snowflake so you can make as many wishes as you can for your family and friends to be happy and hope all their wishes come true.

About the Author

Being born in Anchorage, Alaska, in the army hospital, has always been a nice place to start a wonderful life only going back once at the age of fifty to see where it all started and to run a half marathon.

Being raised in a faith-based family, adventure, humor, and imagination was the foundation which all decisions were made. Spending all summers camping in tents all over the US with two sisters and a brother made for wonderful experiences. Having athletics as a cornerstone was pivotal in shaping valuable sportsmanship values as well as making life-long friendships.

Running cross country, playing tennis, softball, basketball as with all sports promotes positive and healthy competition which will generate a level of confidence that is very powerful.

After miraculously surviving a life-threatening car accident at the age of thirty, coming out of a coma and only ten weeks in the hospital, after regaining some basic memory abilities, learning everything from shapes, colors, and numbers, but learning to walk again was truly the constant faith to overcoming any challenge. Based on the many challenges to overcome from almost dying, walking again, and running the 2000 LA Marathon to be selected to be a torch bearer for the 2002 Winter Olympic Games was profound.

CPSIA information can be obtained
at www.ICGtesting.com
Printed in the USA
BVHW022202130421
604878BV00021B/284